MEET THE GIRL TALK CHARACTERS

Sabrina Wells is petite, with curly auburn hair, sparkling hazel eyes, and a bubbly personality. Sabrina loves magazines, shopping, sleepovers, and most of all, she loves talking to her best friends.

Katie Campbell is a straight-A student and super athlete. With her blond hair, blue eyes, and matching clothes, she's everyone's idea of Little Miss Perfect. But Katie has a few surprises for everyone, including herself!

Randy Zak has just moved to Acorn Falls from New York City, and is she ever cool! With her radical spiked haircut and her hip New York clothes, Randy teaches everyone just how much fun it is to be different.

Allison Cloud is a Native American Indian. Allison's supersmart and really beautiful. But she has one major problem: She's thirteen years old, five foot seven, and still growing!

RANDY'S BIG CHANCE

By L. E. Blair

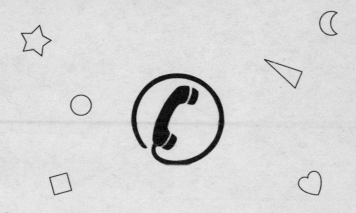

GIRL TALK® series created by Western Publishing Company, Inc.

Western Publishing Company, Inc., Racine, Wisconsin 53404

Text by Katherine Applegate

Chapter One

"Thunder's being a brat today," I told my friends as I leaned forward in my saddle. "Don't be nice to him, you guys."

My three best friends had come to Rolling Hills Stables on Saturday to watch me work with an awesome black stallion named Thunder. I'd been training him for months now — although sometimes I wasn't sure who was training who. Thunder definitely has a mind of his own.

Of course, some people say the same thing about me. My name is Randy Zak.

"Thunder, a brat? I can't believe he's being bad," Sabrina Wells cooed, just like she was talking to a baby. She reached up and stroked Thunder's muzzle. "You're a good horsey, aren't you, Thunder?"

Naturally, Thunder nuzzled her hand like crazy and made little snuffling noises. Putting on his good-horse act. It fakes out most people, but not me. I know the guy too well.

"What did he do that was out of line, Randy?" Allison Cloud asked. She and Katie Campbell were sitting on the fence that ringed the practice area.

"He's been refusing jumps," I complained. "Refusing" is a riding term that means a horse won't jump over something when he's supposed to. Usually Thunder loves to jump. But today he was in one of his moods.

"You don't feel like jumping, do you, boy?" Sabs said, still using baby talk. "Little Thunder doesn't want to jump over all those big old fences."

Thunder turned his black head sideways and gave me an I-told-you-so look.

"Don't give me that look," I said. "You know when you're being bad."

"She's pretty tough," Katie said in a loud whisper that I was definitely supposed to hear.

"Well, you know how Randy is," Allison said with a grin. "All rules and regulations. Everything by the book."

"Very funny," I replied, rolling my eyes.

There's a reason my friends were giving me a hard time. Rules and regulations are about my *least* favorite thing. In fact, some people at Bradley Junior High call me the Queen of Detention. Maybe I do have a *little* bit of an attitude. I guess it's partly because I'm from the city. New York City, to be exact. But when my parents got divorced, my mom wanted to move to someplace totally different. She had grown up in Acorn Falls herself, so one thing led to another, and off we went to the wide-open spaces of Minnesota.

At first I hated it. I couldn't wait to escape.

But then I started getting to know people. Especially Sabrina, Katie, and Allison, my very closest buddies. They weren't anything like the kids I hung out with in New York — or anything like me.

Sabs is a perky redhead who's almost always cheerful and optimistic. I, on the other hand, am not always cheerful and optimistic. And I don't think I've ever been perky. Not even once.

Katie is totally preppie. We're talking plaid skirts, and socks that match the ribbons in her long blond hair. The amazing thing is, she's also the only girl ever to make it onto the boys' hockey team.

I definitely am not the preppie type. I tend to dress in more cutting-edge kinds of styles. And

3

I'm not into anything that might involve being on a team. My sports are skateboarding and horseback riding. You know — solo stuff.

And as for Allison — well, Al is beautiful in an exotic way. She's a Native American. She's incredibly smart and loves to read. And she's much more thoughtful than I am. I definitely admire Al, but I'm not much like her, either.

"Well, I'm going to try and get him to jump one more round," I said, patting Thunder's neck. "Then I'm off to the mall with you guys."

I pulled the reins and turned Thunder into the ring where I had set up our jump. Actually, Richard Cole, this great-looking sixteen-year-old who teaches at the stable, had helped me set up the jump. Richard's parents own the stable — not to mention Thunder.

As I eased Thunder into a trot, I waved to Richard. He was over by the barn, unloading big bales of hay from a truck.

Thunder and I were getting ready to take a jump called a spread. See, a normal jump is just a horizontal rail set on two posts — kind of like a fence, except that if the horse hits the rail, the rail just falls off. That way, the horse doesn't get hurt. A spread is tougher, though, because it's *two* fences a few feet apart. It means the horse has to make a stronger jump, so he can clear both fences.

For some reason, Thunder hates spreads.

I got him up to just the right speed, heading straight for the center of the fence. When they're jumping, a horse and rider really have to work closely together. The rider has to decide how fast the horse should go, and try to get him to exactly the right takeoff point. And if anything about the rider bugs the horse — the way you're sitting or holding the reins — he may misbehave.

We ran toward the fence, closer and closer, until we reached the perfect takeoff point. Suddenly Thunder dug in his heels and stopped dead in his tracks.

This can be very annoying — it's a little like being in a car when the driver slams on the brakes. Only on a horse, you don't have seat belts, and before you know it, you're airborne.

Believe me, that's happened to me more times than I like to remember. Fortunately, this time I managed to stay in the saddle — more or less.

"Fine, Thunder," I muttered, heading him back over to the fence. "Embarrass me in front of my friends."

Suddenly I heard the sound of hooves somewhere behind me. I twisted in the saddle just in time to see a silver-gray horse and its rider entering the ring. The pair approached the jump at exactly the right speed, then flew neatly over the spread and landed perfectly.

"Who was that?" Sabs asked, sounding impressed.

I rolled my eyes. "That's April. You remember — the girl who tried to buy Thunder from Richard's dad?"

"Nice horse," Katie said. "Not as nice as Thunder, of course, but he sure can jump."

I nodded my head glumly. "Yeah, that's Shadowfax. He's a real beauty. Also," I added, giving Thunder a warning look, "he obeys his rider, unlike certain troublesome horses I could name."

I climbed down and led Thunder toward the stable. My friends stayed outside. I think they were afraid I'd try to draft them into helping me groom Thunder. Grooming is what you do after you ride a horse. It's basically cleaning and brushing his coat.

Richard shook his head at Thunder as we passed by. "You're still refusing that spread jump, huh, boy?"

"He's definitely having one of his moods," I said.

Richard nodded thoughtfully. "Try letting him work up a little more speed. Maybe that will help his confidence."

"He wouldn't be a problem if I had trained him," said a voice behind us.

I knew who that had to be. I turned and, sure enough, there was April leading Shadowfax into the stable.

"I was having a private conversation, April," I said curtly. I turned back to Richard. "Thanks for the advice."

Quickly I led Thunder into the stable and tied him to his stall door, trying very hard to ignore April, who was two stalls down.

"You're ruining that horse, you know," April said in her usual superior tone.

I reached down and started loosening the girth, which is the strap that holds the saddle on. "The one time you tried to ride Thunder, he threw you," I reminded her. That had happened several months ago, when I first started taking riding lessons at Rolling Hills. Back then Thunder was so wild that no one could ride him for long, and Mr. Cole had been planning to sell him to April. But after a lot of work and some basic horse psychology, I managed to get Thunder under control. When Mr. Cole saw what a great team we made, he decided to keep Thunder. I don't think April ever really forgave me for that. Ever since then I've been riding at Rolling Hills, and always training with Thunder.

"The only reason he threw me is because he's never been *properly* trained," April snapped. "And he *still* isn't."

I pulled Thunder's saddle off and slung it across the stable door. "How about if you take care of your horse and I take care of mine?" I said.

"He's not your horse," April sneered. "Richard just lets you ride him."

That got me really mad. Maybe because it was true. Sometimes I really felt like he was my horse, and I forgot that he still belonged to Mr. Cole. I wanted to buy Thunder someday, but right now it didn't really seem possible. Even after you buy a horse, you've got to pay for his boarding fees, food, vet care, and so on. It really adds up.

Before I could think of a good comeback for April, Richard came into the barn. He was carrying a clipboard with a bunch of papers attached. He glanced at April, then at me. I think he could tell we'd been arguing.

Without saying anything, Richard pulled one of the blue sheets of paper from his clipboard and handed it to April. Then he came over and handed an identical paper to me.

"What's this?" I asked.

"An entry form for the regional show jumping competition in a few weeks. The preliminaries are in three weeks, and the finals are a week after that."

"Thank you, Richard," April said sweetly.

"Yeah, thanks," I said, wishing he hadn't chosen that exact moment to hand me the entry form. I wondered if April still remembered the vow I'd made a long time ago, when Mr. Cole had decided to keep Thunder. I hadn't just said I was *going* to the regional show jumping competition. Not me. Why do anything halfway? I had to tell the whole world — April included — that I intended to *win* the regionals.

"You're not still thinking about entering, are you?" April asked me. "The competition is only a month away, and the prelims are in just three weeks, and you can't even get your horse over a simple spread. Take my advice, Randy — save yourself the humiliation. Besides, you'll never

beat me and Shadowfax." She shrugged nonchalantly. "A better horse and a better rider."

"No horse is better than Thunder," I said
hotly. But the truth was, I really wasn't sure I
wanted to enter that competition. I had no doubt
that Thunder could beat any horse, when he was
in the mood. I just wasn't so sure *I* could cut it.

"Hey, Ran, if you'd like to take off with your
friends, I'll groom Thunder for you," Richard
said casually. "I still owe you for helping the
other day with Duke." Duke was Richard's
horse. A few days before, I'd groomed Duke
while Richard helped his dad repair a fence.

"That would be great, Richard," I said gratefully. I stroked Thunder's mane one last time and
headed toward the door. I wanted to get out of
there fast before I said something to April that I'd
regret later. Something like, Yes, I am going to
enter the regionals, April, and yes, Thunder and I
are going to blow you away and take home
every blue ribbon in the place.

I was almost out of the barn when I heard
April say loudly to Richard, "I knew she'd chick-
en out."

I tell you, I came this close to turning around
and running back to tell her off. But instead, I just

pretended like I hadn't heard her and walked away.

Chapter Two

"Anyone want this tantalizing, nutritious stuffed gray pepper?" I asked Monday at lunch.

"You mean green pepper," Allison corrected me without looking up from the book she was reading.

"No," I said, poking at it with my fork. "I mean gray. It's *supposed* to be a green pepper, but it's definitely gray."

"Randy, you have no sense of color," Sabs chided, shaking her head disapprovingly. "That's not a gray pepper. It's a brown pepper."

"Would you two stop grossing me out?" Katie complained. "I'm starving, and this is the only thing there is to eat." She cut into the pepper with her fork and looked at it doubtfully. "See? It's green on the inside."

"That's the meat," I pointed out.

"That does it," Sabs said, dropping her fork onto the plate. "This is the last time I ever buy cafeteria food."

Allison reached for her brown-paper lunch bag. "Hmm. Let's see," she said as she looked inside. "A sandwich made with fresh chicken breast, sliced avocado, and sprouts on seven-grain bread. A nice ripe orange. And a chocolate chip brownie. Homemade, of course."

"Of course," I echoed sarcastically.

"I don't suppose you'd consider sharing some of that with those less fortunate?" Sabs asked hopefully.

"Of course I'll share," Al said. "What kind of person do you think I am?" She opened the plastic wrap around her sandwich and carefully pulled out a single sprout. She held it out for Sabs. "Here. It's loaded with vitamin C."

"Your generosity is touching," Sabs said, shooting Al a dirty look.

"Okay, okay," Al said, laughing, as she put the sandwich down on the table. She reached for my knife and neatly cut the sandwich into four equal pieces. We all dived in, and about two and a half seconds later, the sandwich was gone.

"I owe you big-time," I managed to mumble as I chewed. "This sandwich is great. I only wish . . . no, it's too much to ask. Forget it."

"You're not getting my brownie," Al said firmly.

I made a sudden playful grab for it, but Al was too fast and snatched it out of the way. In the process I knocked my notebook with my elbow, sending all my papers flying across the table.

"Oops, this got a little messed up," Sabs said, carefully picking a blue sheet of paper off her plate. "Hope it's not important."

"It's nothing," I said. I hadn't told my friends about the regionals, and I didn't feel much like getting into it now. I reached across the table and grabbed the paper, which was now stained across the middle with stuffed-pepper sauce.

"It looks sort of official," Sabs persisted.

"It's just some announcement from Rolling Hills Stables," I said with a shrug. "I'm on their mailing list."

"So, what is it?" Katie asked.

"It's just an announcement, okay?" I said, a bit louder than I needed to, I guess.

All three of them sat there staring at me quizzically. Oh, well. I was going to have to tell them sooner or later.

"Okay," I said, sighing. "If you must know, it's the entry form for the regional show jumping

14

competition."

"Is that the competition you were going to enter with Thunder?" Katie asked.

I winced. "Maybe."

"Wait a minute," Sabs said in a puzzled tone. "Isn't that the event you challenged that girl April to? You know, where you said you were going to ride Thunder — and win?"

"Okay, I'll share my brownie," Al said quickly. Sometimes Al knows me almost too well. I could tell she was trying to change the subject because she knew the talk about the competition was making me uncomfortable. I had to hand it to her. She was a true friend, sacrificing her brownie in the line of duty.

"Well, maybe just one little bite," I said, giving her a grateful smile.

"So?" Sabs prompted.

The piece of brownie Al had passed me stuck in my throat a little as I tried to swallow. Obviously I wasn't going to weasel my way out of this. Reluctantly I passed the flier back to Sabs.

"Look at this," I said, pointing to the list of rules. "See? Under 'Dress'?"

"Uh-huh," she said, nodding.

"It says traditional dress only."

"So?"

"So, they mean those jodhpur pants and tall leather boots and black jackets and black ties and the whole thing. Plus, the horse's tail has to be braided, and there are certain types of bits you have to use."

"Bits?" Sabs asked me.

Even though she had taken a few riding lessons, she had never been interested much in the little details about tack — all the equipment you need to ride.

"Those metal bars you put in the horse's mouth that are attached to the reins?" I reminded her.

"Oh, right." She nodded. "So, what's the problem?"

"It's just this whole tradition thing. It really bugs me," I said, shaking my head. "All these rules and customs and dress codes. These horse people really get into it, too. People like April."

"Wait a minute," Katie said, giving me a frustrated look. "You mean, you're thinking of backing out of this because of some rules about how you have to dress?"

When I didn't say anything, she just rolled her eyes. To me it was important, even if it did seem dumb to her. When I dress, I make a statement. My own statement — not somebody else's.

"Besides, since when did you let a few rules get in your way?" Sabs added with a laugh.

I thought for a minute. Sabs did have a point. I mean, a competition should be about riding. Not about clothes. Still, it wasn't just the dress requirements that had me worried.

"You know how I sometimes say things before I've totally thought them through?" I asked slowly.

All three smiled, looked at each other, and nodded.

"The truth is, since I made that challenge to April, I've had a lot of time to think the whole competition thing over. And, well, it's expensive, for one thing. I'd have to ride a lot more than I do now, and I do have to pay for that, plus there's the entry fee and stuff. Also . . ." I paused for a moment. "Well, to be honest, Thunder and I just aren't ready. I haven't practiced nearly enough. You guys saw April and Shadowfax the other day. It would be humiliating."

"Come on, Randy. What's the worst that can happen?" Katie asked.

"I could fall on my face."

"It wouldn't be the first time," Katie teased. "And you never know what might happen at the competition. I've gone into some hockey games where I was sure we were going to get creamed, and we've ended up creaming the other team. Remember that game against Monroe?"

I nodded. Our team had come from behind to blow them away in the final seconds.

"Well, all I'm saying is that sometimes when you're the underdog, you take more chances and just cut loose because you don't have anything to lose."

"Still," I argued, "it's one thing when you're part of a team. It's another when it's just you and your horse out there all alone."

Al sighed. "I guess you're right, Ran. April is more experienced, and she does have the more disciplined horse — "

"Give me a break!" I cried. "Thunder could beat Shadowfax with one hoof tied behind his back!"

"Maybe so, but Al's right," Sabs said. "And think how painful it would be to watch April walk away with that blue ribbon." She gave me a pitying look. "Maybe next year, Randy."

I stared at the remains of my pepper. "I know

what you're doing, guys. And child psychology will not work on me."

"Sure," Al said. "We understand. So, when is this competition?" she asked, taking the entry form from Sabs's hand. "Even if you're not in it, I think I might like to go. It should be fun."

"Guys — believe me." I sat back in my chair with my arms across my chest. "This is *not* going to work — "

"Fun to watch April and Shadowfax, you mean?" Sabs piped in as if she hadn't heard a word I'd said. "Well, she's not exactly my favorite person in the world, but it would be neat to watch someone you know win a big tournament like that."

"And she's bound to win, with Randy and Thunder out of it," Katie added in a matter-of-fact tone. "Guess I'll go, too. When is it?"

Katie reached for the flier that Al was still holding, but I sprang up from my seat and got hold of it first.

"All right, it worked. I'll do it," I said, taking the flier back from Al. "Here goes nothing," I said as I smoothed the blue sheet of paper down on the table. My friends looked on with satisfied smiles as I began filling it out.

"Score one for child psychology," Al said triumphantly.

There was only one problem with filling out the entry form for the competition. Before I could send it in, I had to include the entry fee, which was one hundred dollars. I knew how much money I had saved up in the back of my sock drawer, and it wasn't a hundred dollars. It was more like eight dollars. Seven dollars and sixty-five cents, to be exact.

As I skateboarded home from school that afternoon, I thought long and hard about how I was going to convince my mom to part with ninety-two dollars and thirty-five cents.

This wasn't exactly like borrowing a few dollars for a movie. I was going to have to ease into it gradually. Maybe try a little child psychology myself.

When I turned down our street, I was surprised to see the front door to our barn wide open.

Yes, our barn. M (that's what I call my mom, by the way) and I live in a big old converted barn. Inside it's really cool, with high ceilings and skylights, but outside it still has that Farmer Brown look.

I was wondering what was going on, because we don't normally leave our doors wide open. When I reached the barn, I stopped and picked up my board. M came out through the front door, waving her hand back and forth in front of her face.

"Hey, M, what's going on?" I called.

"Oh, it's nothing, really. I was fixing myself lunch and I forgot about it in the oven. And it burned, so it doesn't smell too good in there."

I had to smile. M is not always the most organized person around the house. But then, she's an artist, and artists are supposed to be a little absent-minded. So I wasn't surprised that she'd nuked her lunch. She's also really into health food — all kinds of strange combinations like soybean mush and poached seaweed — so I also wasn't surprised that whatever she'd been cooking smelled bad. It always smelled pretty strange to me.

"How was your day?" M asked. She pulled up one of the lawn chairs and flopped into it. I sprawled out on the grass beside her.

"Cool," I said.

"That's good. I had a pretty cool day, too," she replied, smiling at me. "I finally finished that big canvas."

"The purple-and-black one?" I asked her. M was really working hard lately, getting ready for a show of her paintings at a gallery in Minneapolis. I was really proud of her.

"Uh-huh." She nodded. "Well, it's purple, black, and silver now." She wiggled her fingers, showing off the smears of silver paint.

"Hey, that looks good. I thought you'd gotten some sort of spaced-out manicure," I said.

"Not quite." M laughed and put her head back. She closed her eyes like she was sunbathing.

"Um . . . M?" I said after a few moments. "Can I borrow some money?"

"Is there something you want to buy?"

"Well, kind of," I said evasively. "The regional show jumping competition is coming up."

"Are you going to enter with Thunder?" M opened her eyes and sat up again.

"Well, I'd like to, I guess. Only it's a hundred dollars to enter."

"We can afford that," she said.

I did a double take. I couldn't believe how easily she'd agreed. I should have felt relieved, but for some reason I didn't. I guess I still wasn't totally sure I wanted to be in the competition. If M had just said, "Hey, we can't afford it," the decision would have been made for me.

"Well, there might be some other expenses, too," I added. "Like I'll have to do a lot more practicing. Some of that Mr. Cole will let me work off, but he has to charge something."

M nodded. "That's okay. But when I said we could afford it, Randy, I really did mean *we*. I'll take care of most of it, but I do think it would be good if you could contribute toward the expenses, too."

"I only have seven dollars and sixty-five cents," I admitted. "That's not much of a contribution."

M put her hand to her forehead and closed her eyes. "I sense that more money is coming your way, *very* soon," she said in a mysterious voice. "Yes, the mystic forces tell me that you will soon have an opportunity for greater wealth."

"What are you, psychic all of a sudden?" I asked, laughing.

"No." M grinned. "But just before I burned my lunch, Troy Tanner called up to say he has a gig for your band. He said to call him back as soon as you can."

Troy and I are in a band called Iron Wombat. He's the lead singer and guitarist, and I'm the drummer. We play at teen clubs and at parties, but it had been a while since we'd had a paying job.

"We got a gig?" I jumped up and headed toward the front door. Suddenly I stopped in mid-stride and took a tentative sniff. "Boy, what were you cooking in here?"

"Come on, Ran. It can't be *that* bad."

Actually, it *was* that bad. It was even worse. But I bravely charged inside and headed for the phone to call Troy.

"So, we got a gig," I said as soon as he picked up the phone. "Who with?"

"Hey, kid," Troy said. "Alton handled the whole thing, so I can't tell you much. It's for some girl's party Friday night. About time, huh? I don't know about you, but I'm down to my last pennies."

"Ditto," I said. "I really need the cash."

We talked for a while longer about the gig, but all I could think of was the competition. Now that I could contribute some money, there was no way I could back out. If Thunder and I were going to have a prayer, we were going to have to practice like we'd never practiced before.

"Kid? You there?"

I blinked and realized I'd totally zoned out of

my conversation with Troy. "Sorry," I said. "What were you saying?"

"I was saying that we haven't had a practice in ages. We're really going to have to hustle to make up for lost time."

"I'll say," I agreed.

Making up for lost time was at the top of my list now. But of course, I wasn't thinking about the band.

Chapter Three

The next afternoon after school, I headed straight for the stable. Normally I only go there on weekends, but that morning I had gone ahead and dropped my entry form for the competition in the mailbox. M had lent me the hundred dollars on the condition that I pay her back half as soon as I could. It was official now — I was entered. I didn't have any time to lose.

I saddled Thunder up and got down to business. "Okay, Thunder," I said as we trotted into the ring. "Let's try this one again."

This time as we headed for the spread jump, I took Richard's advice and urged Thunder to greater speed in the approach. We were going pretty fast as we hit the takeoff point, and I found myself bracing for Thunder to refuse again. But suddenly I could feel his front legs lifting, and the coiled power of his hind legs as they propelled us into the air.

There are basically five parts to a jump. The first is called the approach, which is the part where you're cantering toward the fence. Cantering is when the horse is moving at a pace somewhere between a walk and a gallop. Then comes the takeoff, which is pretty much what it sounds like. The takeoff is the hardest part for the rider because you have to shift your weight forward at the exact right moment.

The best part is called the moment of suspension, or just the flight. It only lasts about a second, but it's really great. All of a sudden everything is quiet. You don't hear the horse's hooves pounding, because they're all four off the ground. You don't even hear your own heart pounding — I swear, it more or less stops while you're flying. It's just this incredible, perfect moment. And when you're jumping a spread fence, the flight part lasts just a little bit longer, so it's even better.

Of course, very quickly after the flight comes the landing. That's the scariest part, because you're still leaning way forward and you're sure you're going to go headfirst into the ground.

Finally you have what's called the recovery. That's where, assuming you survived your last jump, you get ready to make your next approach and start all over again.

"Good boy," I said as soon as we had recovered from the jump. "Nice job, Thunder. See? That wasn't so bad, was it?" I kept him cantering along because I didn't want to get him thinking that he could just take it easy after each jump. In a competition there are lots of jumps, and as soon as you're finished with one, you have to be instantly ready for the next.

I rode Thunder around the ring and set him up for another approach to the jump. Once again we built up good speed and flew over with six inches to spare.

"I see Thunder's in a more cooperative mood," Richard said. I hadn't noticed him sitting on the fence and watching. I rode over to him, and Thunder nuzzled his hand.

"He's being a very good boy today. Also," I admitted, "I followed your advice. You were right. I wasn't going into the jump fast enough."

"Later, after he gets more confident about it, you may find he can do it at a lower approach speed just as well," Richard said. "But first Thunder has to be sure he can do it."

"I'm glad I have you to coach me," I said gratefully. "I wouldn't even think about trying to compete if I didn't have your help."

Richard winced and looked down at his boots. "I didn't know that's how you felt, Randy."

"Sure it is. Why shouldn't I?"

"Because I've decided to enter Duke in the advanced class of the competition."

"Cool!"

"Not so cool. I'm really going to have to spend a lot of time practicing. Plus, I still have to keep teaching riding lessons, and handle all my chores. You know how busy my dad keeps me around this place."

"Oh, I get it," I said quietly. "So I guess you won't have a whole lot of time to coach me?"

"Practically no time," Richard said. "I hope this doesn't mean you won't go to the competition. I think you and Thunder could do very well if you work at it."

"Too late for me to decide not to go," I said glumly. "I've already entered."

"That's good. Don't look so depressed."

"But I was already worried about entering. I mean, being humiliated in front of thousands of people isn't my idea of fun. And that competition will be tough. A lot of great riders and great horses will be there."

"Thunder is a great horse," Richard pointed out.

"Yeah, I know he's great. It's his rider I'm not so sure about. Let's face it, April is better than I am."

"Let's face it," Richard echoed with a smile, "lots of riders are better than you are."

"Great! Build up my confidence, coach."

"Randy, you could be a top-notch rider. But you haven't really decided that's what you want to be. April may have less talent than you do, but she's totally committed and . . ." Richard paused.

"And I'm not?" I said, finishing his sentence.

"No, you're not. It takes a lot of work and a lot of practice and a lot of going to competitions where you may not always win."

"I hate not winning," I admitted.

Richard laughed. "I kind of guessed that."

"Great. Now I'm entered in this competition where I'm out of my league and my coach is bailing out on me! I really don't have a chance."

Richard shrugged. "If that's the way you want to look at it."

"How else can I look at it?" I demanded.

"You could decide you're going to succeed, no matter what the odds are against you."

"But you don't think I can win, do you?"

"Randy," Richard said, looking me right in the eye, "sometimes succeeding and winning are not the same thing."

He jumped down off the fence and walked away, leaving me to think about what he'd said. Thunder let out a soft nicker and dipped his head, almost like he was nodding in agreement.

"I'm glad you understood what Richard was talking about," I muttered.

The truth was, I wasn't so sure.

"No, it goes '*da* duh, da duh, duh, duh, *da*,'" I said as I lifted my bass drum into the back of Mr. Tanner's van. It was Friday night, and we were busy stashing all our gear into the minivan Troy's dad had recently bought. Ever since he got it, he's been stuck driving us to all our gigs.

"No way," Troy argued. "It's 'da *duh*, da duh, da, da, *duh*.'"

"Look, you're both wrong," argued Alton, our bass player. "After the first two 'da duhs,' you've got three more."

"Three more what?" I asked.

"Three more 'da duhs,'" Alton explained.

"No way," I said.

"Excuse me, but this is the stupidest conversation I have ever listened to," Jim, our keyboard player, said in an exasperated voice.

We'd been arguing like that for the last half-hour about a brand-new Metal Maniacs song we had just heard on MTV.

"Wait till we get the CD," Troy said confidently. "You'll see I'm right."

"Does your dad have directions to this place?" I asked Troy.

"Sure. It's not far, anyway."

"So, who is this person who's having the party?" I asked.

"Don't know exactly," Alton answered. "I just talked to her dad. He got our number from one of those posters we put up a long time ago. Anyway, his name's Mr. Goodman. I think he said his daughter is turning fourteen or fifteen, or something. One of those ages."

Goodman? The name sounded awfully familiar to me. Then I realized why. April's last name was Goodman. Could her birthday party possibly be our gig? That would be a nightmare come true. Goodman is a pretty common name, I told myself. It doesn't have to be April's party.

"So, does she go to Bradley?" I asked Troy,

hoping to figure out if it was April or not.

"Who cares if she goes to Bradley?" Troy said as he climbed into the van behind me. Mr. Tanner started up the motor and we took off. "We play the same music, no matter what school she goes to."

And I was hoping that, whoever she was, she *wasn't* April.

We pulled up to the Goodman house and started unloading our equipment. The garage door was open, and a man came out to meet us. I had seen April's father a few times at the stable, and this man was definitely not him.

"Hi," I said in a friendly tone. "Are you Mr. Goodman?"

The man stared at me a second, then sort of laughed. "Not quite. I'm Mr. Delicious." He pointed to a van in the garage. I could see the words MISTER DELICIOUS — GOURMET FOODS painted on the side. "The caterer."

"Oh, right." I nodded. "Nice to meet you. We're Iron Wombat."

"Of course you are," he said cheerfully. "Just follow me. I'm glad you kids got here on time."

Mr. Delicious seemed to be in a rush. We really had to move to keep up with him as he led us through the house to a very large room near the back. All the furniture had been removed, and the caterer's helpers were setting up tables along one side.

There was a small raised stage at the far end of the room, so we headed over there to set up. Of course, being the drummer, it always takes me the longest. Not only do I have to set up my drums, I have to arrange the microphones around them. Troy's got it easiest. He just plugs in his guitar and adjusts the voice mike to the right height, and he's ready to rock.

It took us about an hour to get everything ready. And just about every second of that hour, I was silently wishing that it wasn't April's house.

Finally I knew for sure when a familiar voice beside me said, "What are *you* doing here?"

I looked up from the snare drum I'd been positioning. My wishes had definitely *not* been answered. It was April, dressed in the height of snooty-preppie fashion.

"I'm with the band," I replied. "I'm the drummer, see?" I stood up and waved the sticks at her.

"Well, I hope you're better at drumming than you are at riding," April said coolly.

"You girls know each other, I guess?" Troy

said.

"We ride at the same stable," I explained.

"One of us rides," April corrected me. "The other person just thinks she does."

I climbed down off my stool and walked to the front of the stage. We'd been hired to play at this girl's party. It would be unprofessional of me to tell off the guest of honor. But it sure was tempting.

"Look, April, I know you don't think much of my riding," I said. "But it's your birthday and all, so why don't we just call a truce for tonight and have a good time?"

"You're right," April replied. I turned back toward my drums. However, April wasn't ready to give up. "I *don't* think much of your riding. Riding is a sport for gentlemen and ladies. Not for people like you. I've heard that you're in detention more than any other girl at Bradley."

It was true that I held the record. But I didn't need April broadcasting the news all over town for me. I had tried to be cool, but she was definitely starting to make me mad.

I climbed down off the stage so I could look her right in the eye. "I think you're just afraid of me," I said, doing my best to look intimidating. I was pleased when she took a step back. "In fact, I think you can't stand the idea that Thunder and I might beat you in that competition."

To my surprise, she laughed. It wasn't a fake laugh, either. She really thought what I had said was funny.

"Get real, Randy," she said. She was still laughing a little and just shook her head. "You don't have a prayer. If you even get through the preliminaries, it will be because you have a great horse. It certainly won't be because of your riding skill."

That really burned me — maybe because I halfway thought she might be right.

"Face it," April continued. "You've got a great horse, but that's all you've got." She shook her head. "You don't even have a trainer, do you?"

"I've got Richard —" Sort of, I added to myself.

"Richard's okay, but he's no George Quillen."

"I take it I'm supposed to know this George dude?"

"He's only a former Olympic gold medalist in show jumping," April said with a tilt of her chin. "And he just happens to be my trainer."

"I guess you can use all the help you can get,"

I replied.

"Good one, Randy," April replied with a laugh. "You're pretty funny," she admitted. "But it will take more than wisecracks to win the regionals."

I have to admit, she had me stumped there. For once I couldn't even think of a clever comeback.

Troy walked down to the edge of the stage and squatted down to talk to us. "Are you girls done chatting?" he asked. "Because I think the guests are like starting to wonder why there's a band standing up here but no music."

"Sure, you can start playing," April said with a shrug. "Randy and I are done talking." Then she turned on her heel and took off across the room to greet some of her guests.

"What was that all about?" Troy asked me.

"It's sort of hard to explain." I looked at him and shook my head. "Let's just get this gig going already, okay?"

"Hey, fine with me, kid. Let's rock."

I hopped up on the stage and got behind my drums again. April had really gotten under my skin. In fact, I was so steamed up, I felt about ready to explode. Luckily, that was a perfect mood for playing drums with Iron Wombat.

In fact, after the first set Troy gave me one of his rare compliments and said my playing was really stellar. The rest of the night went just as well, and we really rocked the place. When I got home, I felt good about the gig.

Still, April's comment had really gotten under my skin, and that night I lay in bed wondering if maybe there was something in what she'd said to me. Maybe I *didn't* belong in the horseback riding set. It was full of snobs. People like April, who were into tradition and formality and breeding — the kind of stuff that really turns my stomach.

Besides, she was probably right about my chances at the competition. I hadn't really been riding all that long, compared to April. If I'd been into betting, I wouldn't have bet on me to win, that's for sure.

If only I had kept my megamouth shut about the competition. Now I could either back out of the whole thing and look like a coward, or go through with it and be humiliated in front of thousands of people.

Great choice.

By the next morning I wasn't feeling much better, even though it was Saturday. I got out of bed

late and cruised downstairs to find M already finishing her health food breakfast — some grainy
brown stuff sprinkled over some lumpy white
stuff. I didn't bother to ask what it was. I was
afraid that she might decide it was just what I
needed to start off the day.

"Morning," I said, yawning.

"Good morning. How did the party go last
night?"

"We were great. But the girl who gave the
party was a dweeb."

M smiled. "Did the dweeb's parents pay
you?"

"Yeah. Mr. Goodman even tipped us extra. He
was cool."

"That was nice of him," M said. "How about a
high-energy breakfast, Ran? I bet you just gorged
yourself on junk food last night."

M was right. I had pigged out at the buffet
table at April's party. Mr. Delicious's food really
lived up to his name. But luckily, before I had to
fend off a bowl of high-energy health mush, the
phone rang.

"I'll get it," I offered. I jumped up from my seat
and grabbed the phone. M just stared at me. I
guess she couldn't figure out what was going on,

because I'm usually so slow moving in the morning.

"Zak residence," I said.

"Morning, Randy. This is a call from the Zak-mobile," a familiar voice answered with a chuckle. "What's happening out there in the wide-open spaces?"

"Hey, D!" I just about yelled. D is what I call my dad. The Zakmobile is what I call his car, because he has all these electronic gadgets in it — a phone, a fax, even a CD player. "Not much on this end, D. But there's still a lot of space out here to happen in."

That answer made D laugh. Truth was, I wasn't up to all that much. Unless you counted the jumping competition. I hadn't really planned on telling D about it, but I didn't have much else to say. There was the party last night. And I'd gotten an A-minus on my last Italian quiz. Hardly headline news. So, like an idiot, I told him all about the competition.

"Did you say it's in three more weeks?" D asked.

"That's the date of the finals. If I make it that far." And that's a big if, I added to myself.

"I'm going to be there," D said firmly.

"What?"

"I said, I'm going to be there. I want to see you ride."

Now, maybe I should explain two things. First, I really love my dad, and miss him. I think he's totally cool, as dads go. Second, he's very busy, so it's a major thing when he can get time away from his work.

Normally, nothing would make me happier than having D come for a visit. Unless, of course, he was coming to watch me make a fool of myself.

"Oh, you don't have to bother, D," I said casually.

"What do you mean, 'bother'? You're my favorite person on planet Earth, Randy, and I have some time off. Who else should I spend my time with?"

Well, he had me there. It wasn't like I could say, "Stay home, D. Don't come." That's what I wanted to say, but even I know you can't just say everything that pops into your brain.

"That would be great, D," I said. I tried to sound enthusiastic, but my head was filled with pictures of him sitting in the stands as his daughter went flying through the air and fell on her head.

"Tell your mom, okay? I'll stay in Minneapolis and meet you guys there at the stadium."

"D, I could still get eliminated in the preliminaries, you know."

"No way. Forget about it. I'll see you there."

"Cool," I said as I hung up the phone, although cool was not at all how I felt.

Chapter Four

Randy calls Allison.

ALLISON: Hello, Cloud residence.

RANDY: Al, thank goodness you're home.

ALLISON: Hey, Randy. What's up?

RANDY: D!

ALLISON: D?

RANDY: My dad. He's coming.

ALLISON: Cool!

RANDY: No, it is definitely *not* cool.

ALLISON: Since when? I thought you loved it when your dad comes to visit.

RANDY: I do. But he's not just coming for a visit. He's coming to watch me ride in that *stupid* competition.

ALLISON: That's not good?

RANDY: Al, I'm probably going to get wiped out. Destroyed. Beaten. Whipped.

ALLISON: Don't you think Thunder can win?

RANDY: Thunder's great. I'm the one who's not ready. A lot of these other riders have been riding for years. They own their own horses, and they've taken lessons since they were three years old.

ALLISON: I thought it had more to do with who has the best horse.

RANDY: *(Sighs)* That's what people always think. But every move the rider makes is important, too. Like if I lean forward too soon in the take-off, I may cause him to lose his balance. Or if I don't lean forward soon enough, I can catch him in the mouth —

ALLISON: Catch what?

RANDY: Catch him in the mouth. See, when a horse jumps, he stretches forward. If the rider's still leaning back, holding on to the reins, the horse thinks the rider's pulling back on the reins to make him stop and he gets totally confused.

ALLISON: *(Pauses)* I didn't realize that it was so complicated. Do you actually

	know all this stuff?
RANDY:	That's just my point. I barely know any of it. It was bad enough that I was going to be humiliated in front of all my friends and a whole stadium full of strangers. Now I have to make a fool of myself in front of D, who is going to fly over a thousand miles just so he can watch me be a dork.
ALLISON:	I don't think you're going to look like a dork. You may not win, but I've seen you ride, and you are definitely good, Ran.
RANDY:	Thanks. *(Pauses)* I guess.
ALLISON:	Look, I know you said Richard's going to be busy, but I'm sure he can give you a few pointers here and there, can't he?
RANDY:	He said he wouldn't have much time at all, Al. *(Sighs)* April's got some gold-medal trainer, did I tell you that? But I guess I'm on my own.
ALLISON:	You're never on your own, Ran. I'll always be there to help.

RANDY: You're a true pal, Al. But you're no riding coach.

ALLISON: I guess not.

RANDY: Hey, what if I just pretend to have the flu? Then April can't say I was a coward, and I'll have a perfect excuse for not showing up. No one will know.

ALLISON: You'll know.

RANDY: True. But maybe I can live with the fact that I'm a coward.

ALLISON: Don't give up yet, Randy. Maybe something will happen to change everything. Are you going out to the stable today?

RANDY: Yeah, I guess so. I'm not really up for it, but Thunder will be expecting me.

ALLISON: Why don't we all go to Fitzie's first? Then afterward, we can watch you ride and give you moral support.

RANDY: Why not? I might as well get used to having people laugh at me.

ALLISON: See you at Fitzie's.

RANDY: I'm on my way.

Allison hangs up and calls Katie.

KATIE: Cam-fm-lmf.

ALLISON: Katie? Is that you?

KATIE: Mmhm. Mm. Okay, that's better. Sorry, I had a mouthful of peanut butter.

ALLISON: Listen. I just got off the phone with Randy, and she's totally bummed over this riding competition.

KATIE: Really? Why?

ALLISON: Her dad's flying in from New York to watch her, and she thinks she stinks. She's really worried about not having anyone to help her train.

KATIE: Just between you and me, she probably should be worried.

ALLISON: What's the big deal about having a coach? She's a great rider and Thunder's a great horse.

KATIE: Look, I'm a good skater, but I couldn't play hockey as well if I didn't have a coach. You need someone who can watch you practice and tell you what you do wrong. See, when you're doing something — playing hockey or riding a horse — you're too busy doing it to think about *how* you're doing it.

ALLISON: Oh. So Randy isn't just exaggerating? This really is bad?

KATIE: I guess it depends on how good some of the other riders are. That's why we always watch a game film.

ALLISON: What's a game film?

KATIE: Someone videotapes our game, then we watch the video and see how we did, and how the other team did, too.

ALLISON: I wonder if that would help Randy?

KATIE: What? A game film?

ALLISON: Sure. Someone could videotape her practicing with Thunder, and then she could look at it later.

KATIE: I guess it would be better than nothing. Especially if she can get a tape of a really great rider and compare the two. But who's going to videotape Randy?

ALLISON: I think I know. Thanks, Katie! Great idea. I have to hang up now. Oh — don't eat any more peanut butter. We're hitting Fitzie's soon.

KATIE: Uh . . . okay. Whatever you say. Bye, Al.

Allison calls Sabrina.

SABRINA: Wells residence.

ALLISON: Does your dad still have a video-camera?

SABRINA: Sure. But why?

ALLISON: It's a long story. Do you think he'd let you borrow it?

SABRINA: I think so.

ALLISON: Can you meet us at Fitzie's in an hour or so?

SABRINA: What's going on?

ALLISON: We're going to be coaches.

Chapter Five

When Sabs, Katie, and Al showed up at Fitzie's that afternoon armed with a camcorder, I have to admit I had my doubts about the whole idea. But Katie seemed to think watching tapes had really helped her hockey game, and the more I thought about it, the more I figured, What can it hurt?

If I really wanted to go all the way with the plan, I had to get some tapes of championship riders from the library. It would be painful to compare myself to them, but as my "coaches" told me, "No pain, no gain."

When we got to the stable, Thunder turned out to be a real ham. He pranced around in front of the camera, strutting his stuff, and every time Sabs started rolling the film, his ears pricked up. Once he even tried to eat the lens.

On Sunday evening we all got together at my place to watch the video of Thunder and me in action. M and her boyfriend, Terry Murphy, who's a history teacher at the high school, decided to stick around and watch, too. Terry helped me pop up a bunch of microwave popcorn while M dimmed the lights and everyone else settled in front of the TV.

"Now, remember, this is my first stab at making a movie," Sabs warned as she popped the tape in the VCR.

"Hey, wait for the star of the show!" I yelled from the kitchen as Terry and I began pouring the popcorn into bowls.

"Take your time, Ran. There's some practice stuff at the beginning of the tape," Sabs said, sounding a little apologetic.

Suddenly everyone in the living room burst into laughter. From where I was standing in the kitchen, I couldn't see the TV screen, so I had no idea why they were all cracking up.

"All right!" Katie hooted. "I give this a thumbs-up for sure!"

"Gross," Al moaned. "I want a refund on my ticket."

"You didn't tell us this was X-rated, Sabs," M teased.

Terry gave me a jab with his elbow. "Just what

exactly did you film yesterday, anyway?"

"I'm afraid to find out," I said, tossing him the bag of popcorn I'd just pulled out of the microwave.

I dashed into the living room just in time to see Sabs's twin brother, Sam, right there in living color on our TV screen — mooning us.

"That's the ugliest horse I've ever seen," I remarked.

"Sorry," Sabs said, her cheeks flaming. Sabs blushes at the drop of a hat.

"Just promise me this," I said, dropping onto the couch next to Al. "That's it for the sneak preview of Sam, right?"

Sabs crossed her hand over her heart. "I swear. Right after he flashed the camcorder, my mom made him go clean out the garage as punishment." She pointed to the screen. "From now on, it's all stuff I taped at the stable."

Terry came in, carrying two heaping bowls of popcorn. "Did I miss something?" he asked.

"Should I reverse the tape for Terry?" Sabs laughed.

"NO!" we all shouted in unison.

Suddenly a shot of Al, Katie, and me appeared on the screen. The camera was jiggling so much, it took me a minute to realize that we were sitting at our usual table at Fitzie's.

"Wait a minute," I said. "That's not the stable, either." I turned to Sabs. "You took shots of us porking out on Fitzburgers?"

Sabs tilted her chin. "That's called artistic license, Randy. I am the director, after all. I was just trying to capture you in your, um . . ."

"Natural element?" Terry offered.

"Exactly!" Sabs said.

"You're supposed to be helping me with my technique," I complained, tossing a throw pillow at Sabs.

"But you *have* great technique, Randy," Al said, nodding at the screen. "Look at the way you handle those fries!"

"I don't know, Al," Katie said doubtfully. "I think her takeoff into the catsup was a little late."

"Great," I muttered, crossing my arms over my chest. "You're not the ones putting your butt on the line."

"No, Sam took care of that," M remarked.

"There!" Sabs said excitedly, pointing to the screen. "There's Thunder now!"

"Finally," I said with a loud sigh.

The camera panned — well, jostled, is more

like it — to a shot of me feeding Thunder a carrot. You could hear me whispering things to him, but mostly what you heard was his very loud munching. Thunder has lousy table manners.

"Awww," M murmured as Thunder nuzzled my cheek.

"There they are," Sabs said. "Beauty and the Beast."

"Thunder *is* beautiful, isn't he?" Katie said with a laugh.

She turned around to check my reaction, so naturally, I did the only thing I could do — I tossed the other throw pillow on the couch at her and scored a direct hit.

"Look!" M cried as the scene changed to the practice ring.

I looked at the screen and saw Thunder and me approaching our first set of jumps. You could tell from my expression that I didn't have anything on my mind but making a clean jump. Thunder was just as focused — his mane streaming, his nostrils flaring, his eyes glued on the goal ahead of us.

"He is beautiful," I whispered. It was the first time I'd had the chance to see us working together, and I felt this rush of excitement. We were a pair, a team —

Suddenly we flew over the first spread and the room fell silent, all of us watching as Thunder took me for a ride in the sky. Our landing wasn't bad — my timing was a little off, maybe, but Thunder kept his stride and took the next jump easily.

Not bad, I told myself. Maybe we could handle the prelims, after all. It wasn't exactly gold-medal-at-the-Olympics time, but all in all, I was surprised at how good we'd looked.

Sabs pushed the STOP button, and everybody gave me a round of applause.

"Randy!" M exclaimed. "That was incredible!"

"Thunder does all the work," I said with a shrug. "I just try to stick around for the ride."

"It was a great jump," Katie said. She paused. "Although — "

"Although what?" I asked.

"Well, what do I know?" Katie said with a shrug. "You're the expert."

"No, really," I said. "That's the whole idea here. I need all the help I can get if I'm going to survive the prelims."

"It's just that I thought maybe your takeoff was maybe a tiny bit late," Katie said gently.

"Late?" Al demanded. "I thought it was early."

"I don't know about all this takeoff stuff," M said, "but I was wondering about the way you leaned forward in the beginning. Are you supposed to do that, or were you just afraid of losing your balance?"

"Well — " I began, but Terry interrupted me before I could get going.

"Did you see the way the horse's hooves almost touched the second fence?" Terry asked. "Maybe you should ask him to jump a little higher, Ran. You know — just to be on the safe side."

"Um . . . sure," I said, nodding at all of them. I was starting to have my doubts about this whole video session. I mean, I was trying to improve my technique, but getting free advice from a bunch of rank amateurs wasn't exactly doing wonders for my confidence.

"You know the only thing that was wrong with that jump?" Sabs asked.

I crossed my arms over my chest. "No," I said, "but everyone else seems to."

"We're just trying to be helpful, hon," M put in.

"It's not the way you jumped," Sabs said with a grin. "It's what you were wearing. I'm telling you, Ran — some jodhpurs and one of those little black hats, and you're going to look just as professional as everyone else at the prelims."

"Oh, I love all those horsey clothes," M said. "Those jackets like the kind Elizabeth Taylor wore in *National Velvet*. And those puffy pants — "

"I am not wearing jodhpurs when I can wear jeans," I said firmly. "They make it look like you've got thighs the size of the Goodyear Blimp."

"I don't think you exactly have a choice on this," Al said. "Everybody at the prelims will be wearing the same thing. And don't forget what the entry form said about required dress."

"Forget it," I said firmly. "I wouldn't be caught dead in one of those getups. Besides, I don't think they care as much about what you wear to the prelims as they do about your clothes for the finals." I nodded to Sabs. "Play the rest of the tape, would you, Sabs?"

"Could we at least go to the tack shop next weekend and look at some clothes?" Sabs asked.

"Roll it, Sabs," I commanded, shaking my head.

She pushed the PLAY button and the screen came back to life. It took me a moment to realize that the next scene was showing April and Shadowfax as they approached the same spread.

"You said to get some other people on tape so you could compare," Sabs reminded me.

I nodded, my eyes glued to the screen. April and Shadowfax took their approach and sailed cleanly over the spread. I slumped back against the couch and sighed. It was beautiful. Flawless. They made it look effortless, like a little trot through Central Park.

"Big deal," Al said. "You and Thunder were just as good."

"Al's right," Katie chimed in. "Your jump looked just the same."

"Thanks, guys," I said gratefully. "But let's face it — she's better."

Sabs froze the tape. "April is not a better rider," she insisted, shaking her finger at me. "She just *looks* like a better rider."

"Come on, Randy," Katie urged. "Let's go clothes shopping next Saturday. What can it hurt?"

I stared at the TV screen. April and Shadowfax stared back at me, frozen in mid-stride. I had that horrible, deep-in-your-gut feeling you get when you know you've gotten yourself into something and it's way too late to get out of it.

"Okay," I muttered, "I'll go. But I'm not making any promises. And no jodhpurs."

All week I practiced really hard at the stable. I showed up every single day after school and rode till dark. My homework may have suffered a bit, but I figured it was all for a good cause.

I'd planned to spend all day Saturday and Sunday with Thunder. But my friends, it turned out, had other ideas. At ten on Saturday morning I found myself being dragged through a store called Cowgirl Blues. And I do mean dragged.

"Here's the deal," I said as Sabs paused in front of a rack of black riding jackets. "No jodhpurs. No gloves. No tie. No — "

"Look at this one," Sabs interrupted, holding out a tailored black jacket. "Just try it on for size."

Reluctantly I tried on the coat. "Why would anyone want to ride in this?" I demanded, gazing at my reflection in a nearby full-length mirror. I stretched out my arms the way I would if I was holding on to Thunder's reins. "It's tight," I complained, shucking off the jacket impatiently. "I feel a lot more comfortable in my own clothes, where I can really move if I need to."

"But you know everybody wears this stuff, Randy," Al said. "It's traditional."

"So I'm a rugged individualist," I said, shoving the jacket back on a hanger. "Tradition stinks."

A tall, primly dressed woman yanked the jacket out of my hands. Her name tag read PHILIPPA. "Let me take care of that for you, dear," she said pointedly. She gave me a quick up and down. "Saddle seat or forward seat?"

"Excuse me?" I said.

"What do you ride? Saddle or forward? It will determine how you dress."

"Oh, I jump," I said.

"Forward seat, then."

"But I already know what I'm wearing."

"She's going to be in the regional show jumping prelims," Sabs volunteered.

"How nice," Philippa said. Suddenly she seemed a lot more friendly. I could tell she thought she had a live one, so I figured it was only fair to straighten her out.

"But at the prelims I'm just going to wear my lucky T-shirt and a pair of jeans," I explained quickly.

Philippa threw back her head and laughed loudly. Me, I wasn't quite sure what the punchline was. "Let's hit the road, guys," I began, but suddenly Philippa grabbed me by my shoulders.

"Just you leave her to me," she said to my friends. "Give me ten minutes alone with — what was your name, dear?"

"Randy," Al said, grinning widely.

"Don't worry, Randy," Philippa said to me with another toothy smile. "We'll make an equestrian out of you yet." She made little sweeping motions with her hands at my friends. "Come back in ten minutes, girls. You won't believe your eyes."

I couldn't believe my eyes, either. My three best friends ran off instantly, leaving me in Philippa's clutches. Normally I would have put up more of a fight, but I guess I was a little curious to see how I'd look in the whole outrageous getup she had planned for me.

Ten minutes later I knew.

I looked like a complete, total, disgusting riding weasel.

Philippa hadn't missed a trick. I got the complete treatment — black jacket, tan jodhpurs, white shirt, black tie, white gloves, and high black boots. The outfit was topped off by a black derby — a round hard hat with a chin strap. It was the only piece of official horse garb I already owned. You really had to wear one just in case the horse acted up and you were thrown.

"Randy!" Sabs exclaimed as she and the others returned to find me standing, horrified, in front of a mirror. "You look incredible!"

"I look like one of those superhorsey types at the stable."

"A flower in the buttonhole is always a nice touch," Philippa said, reaching over to adjust my tie.

I gave her a pleading look. "A *flower*?"

"Optional, of course," Philippa added quickly.

"It's all optional as far as I'm concerned," I said, ripping off the derby. "This isn't me. I can't even breathe in this outfit, much less do everything I have to do when I'm riding Thunder. Sorry, gang. I'm sticking with jeans."

"But, Randy — " Sabs began.

"This just isn't how it's done, dear," Philippa argued.

"But it's how *I* do it," I replied, and I handed her back the hat.

Chapter Six

I spent the next week the same way I'd spent the last one — practicing like crazy. It had begun to pay off. At least I thought it had. I was feeling a lot more confident and relaxed. I was even beginning to think we had a shot at surviving the preliminaries.

That is, until I arrived at the site for the prelims early Saturday morning. Seeing the course laid out as I drove up with M, I felt my stomach do some serious gymnastics. Even from a distance, I could tell it was going to be tough.

The prelims were being held at the grounds where they had the county fair each year, and I tried to console myself that at least the viewing stands were a lot smaller than they would be at the regional competition in Minneapolis.

M parked the car and we both got out. "I guess I'd better go find the Coles," I said.

Mr. Cole and Richard had transported

Thunder and Richard's horse, Duke, in their double-horse trailer.

"I'll go find a seat near your friends," M said. "See you later."

"See you," I said, with a nervous smile. Well, at least I had a few fans in the crowd, I thought as M headed off toward the stands.

A few minutes later, I found the Coles' horse trailer near the stable. Richard had already begun unloading the horses, and I quickly offered to help him.

"So, are your ready for the meet?" Richard asked me as he gave Duke a soothing pat and eased him out of the trailer.

"Not exactly, but here I am," I said with a shrug.

"You call that positive thinking?" he asked.

"I call it realistic thinking," I replied grimly.

It took me a couple of tries to get Thunder out of the trailer. Horses are not big road-trip fans. I guess they figure, Why ride in some gas-guzzling contraption when you've got all the horsepower you need?

While Richard kept an eye on Duke and Thunder, I headed over to the ring to check out the situation and pace off the jumps. It's called walking the course, and all the riders do it.

Carefully I paced off the distance between each of the fences. There were a total of nine fences set up in the ring. Most were your basic verticals. A vertical is just like a piece of a fence. Sometimes the fences are made from striped poles, sometimes from old logs, and some look like white-painted gates. Then there are the spreads. They are two vertical fences set one in front of the other, either at the same height or at different heights.

Whatever they're made of, all these fences are built so that the rails can be easily knocked down if the horse happens to hit them. That way the horse's legs don't get banged too much. It also makes it easier for the judges to tell when a horse has hit one of the rails. Knocking one of the rails down is called a knockdown.

I looked at the distance between the second and third fences, trying to get it straight in my mind so I would remember later. A distance of twenty-four feet meant that Thunder could only take one step between the second and third jumps.

Once I had that straight in my head, I walked the distance between the third fence, which was a vertical, and the fourth fence, which was a spread. This was thirty-four feet, which meant Thunder could take two steps between them.

I shook my head. Already I was confused. There was no way I was going to be able to keep all of it straight.

By the time I'd gotten to the sixth fence, I was feeling totally crazed. I mean, okay, it had helped to be able to watch myself and Thunder on video, and to compare the tape to one showing a really expert rider. And I'd been practicing as hard as I could. But who was I kidding? I still didn't feel confident.

"This is the spot," April said, breaking in on my gloomy thoughts.

She was standing by the sixth fence, which was the highest vertical in the course. She was impeccably dressed in cream-colored jodhpurs, polished leather riding boots, and a black jacket. And she was grinning.

"What?" I demanded.

"I said, this is the spot. Right here. You come off jump number five and you have to turn the horse sharply to the left and set up quickly for the next jump."

"So?"

"So, it's a maneuver that requires a confident, experienced rider. Otherwise the horse will sense that you're uncertain and will refuse the jump. That's why I said, 'This is the spot.' Because this is the spot where you will lose it totally."

She grinned that infuriating, superior grin of hers and walked away.

I wanted to shout something at her retreating back, but nothing came to mind. Nothing but fear. She was right. It was a tough jump, and she had spotted it instantly. It hadn't even looked like any big deal to me, but that was because I was inexperienced.

I stood there at the sixth fence for a while, pretending to be very carefully pacing off the distance, but to tell the truth, all I could think about was how April was right. Thunder would refuse.

I left the ring without even looking at the last three jumps, and found M and my friends all gathered around Thunder. Richard had moved him into a stall in the stable at the edge of the fairgrounds.

"Hey, Randy," Al called out as she caught sight of me. "How did it look?"

I swallowed hard. "Fine. No problem."

"Good," Sabs said, sounding relieved,

"because it looked really hard to me. All those jumps! And some of them are really high. One even looks like it's taller than me."

"Uh-huh," I said distractedly. "Well, guys, I better get Thunder over to the warm-up area."

I noticed M and Al both looking at me quizzically. Just my luck that the two people who can read me like a book were there.

"Remember, honey," M said, "it's supposed to be fun."

"Really, Ran. It's not like the fate of the world is hanging in the balance," Al added with an encouraging smile.

Obviously they were trying to loosen me up, which meant they thought I was tense, which just made me even more tense.

I opened Thunder's stall and led him out.

"Good luck, Randy," Katie said cheerfully. "Remember our game with Monroe!"

"I'll try," I said lamely. It was about all the self-confidence I could manage.

In the warm-up ring there were two fences set up so that people could take their horses over a couple of fairly easy jumps and get them in the mood. I got there just in time to see Shadowfax and April go flying over the first fence with about eight inches to spare.

"Don't let it shake you, boy," I told Thunder, patting the side of his neck. "He's good, but you're better." I was sure of that, at least.

I climbed into the saddle and led him around the ring in a trot. There were a dozen other horses there, so naturally Thunder had to try to break into a gallop to show all of them how fast he was. I kept him in check, but just barely. Then, as soon as it looked clear, I took him toward the first jump. We cleared it like it wasn't even there, which made me feel a little better.

Suddenly the loudspeaker blared with the name of the first rider. I walked Thunder over to the fence by the main ring so we could watch. It's always good if you're not the first rider, because that way you can watch some of the other people and see where they have trouble. Hopefully, you can learn from their mistakes.

The first guy was a dude with a beautiful roan mare. They got into trouble right away. They cleared the first fence, but then the mare refused the second fence. She jumped it on the second approach but knocked down a rail.

I was sorry for the guy and his horse, but at the same time, I have to admit I felt a little relieved. At least I wouldn't be the only one to mess up. Besides, I had four other people going before me. That meant I had plenty of time to get Thunder loosened up. Maybe the day wouldn't be a total disaster, after all.

Just then I heard a horse sidling up alongside us. I didn't turn to look, but then, I didn't really have to. I recognized the horse's head as he gave Thunder a look.

"You'd better hurry," April said in a helpful, friendly voice. "You don't have much time to change into your riding clothes."

"I'm in my riding clothes," I snapped.

April laughed. "But you can't possibly be. One doesn't wear blue jeans to a competition."

"One does if one is me," I said.

"Do you see anyone else wearing blue jeans?" April demanded, waving her arm toward the other riders. I could tell that several of them were eavesdropping on the conversation.

I scanned the group, and sure enough, everyone else — including Richard — was wearing your basic jodhpurs and black riding jacket. April was totally maxed out in snob horse clothing. I was wearing jeans and this great sweater my dad sent me from my favorite shop in New York. I looked great. But I did look . . . different.

"The entry form didn't say anything about having to wear the whole monkey suit at the preliminaries — just the finals." Maybe that wasn't entirely true — but, hey, April was getting on my nerves big-time.

Again April came up with that know-it-all laugh of hers. "It's assumed." Then she just shrugged. "Suit yourself, but I doubt if the judges will be pleased with your fashion statement, Randy."

"I didn't know this was a fashion show, April. I thought we were here to ride," I replied. Then I was mad at myself for even showing a reaction.

I don't know what it was. Normally I have no trouble blowing off snobs like April. But for some reason I couldn't manage to ignore her. Maybe it was the fact that even though she was a jerk, she really did know how to ride.

"Next up, Randy Zak from Acorn Falls, riding Thunder of Rolling Hills Stables."

When the announcement came over the loudspeaker, I nearly panicked again. It still wasn't too late to just take Thunder back to his trailer, get in the car with M, and head on home. I would be a coward, but maybe that was better than what I was about to be.

"Remember," April said, "the sixth fence."

Without a word or even a glance in April's direction, I urged Thunder toward the entrance to the main ring. Out in the crowd, I heard someone cheering for me.

I was supposed to stop in front of the judges' box and salute them, but I was too freaked to remember.

"Here goes nothing," I muttered as we headed into the ring. I tried to concentrate on the first fence like you're supposed to. You know — block everything else out of your mind. But the truth was, it was all turning into a big blur. I could barely focus on where the first fence was, let alone think about the timing of my approach or the number of paces between fences.

I breathed deeply a few times, and we just took off. We were flying over the first fence before I even realized what was happening. Thunder took two paces, then sailed over the second fence.

"The sixth fence, that's the one," I muttered.

On the third fence I nearly lost it. I was too late leaning forward and ended up yanking back on the reins, just trying to hold on. This made Thunder pull back his head, and I heard the depressing sound of his rear hooves knocking down the top rail.

I tried to get my concentration back for the fourth fence, but this time I leaned into the jumping position too early. Fortunately, Thunder managed to make it, even with my lousy riding.

"Here it comes," I said under my breath.

Thunder cantered toward the fifth jump. I knew that as soon as we landed, we had to make a sharp left turn. April's words kept going round and round in my head.

Thunder gathered his hind legs under him and cleared the fifth fence. As soon as we hit the ground, I tried to turn him.

It was too soon! I could tell he was unbalanced and confused. He took a second, stumbling stride toward fence number six and stopped dead in his tracks. I nearly fell out of the saddle. I only managed to hang on because I grabbed his mane.

"Hang in there, boy," I whispered. I turned Thunder around, and we headed again toward fence number six. This time he jumped, and we cleared it.

Thunder cleared fence seven, but had a knockdown on fence eight. We cleared the final fence with room to spare.

There wasn't exactly a standing ovation from the crowd. I knew we'd blown it. Badly. One refusal and two knockdowns. It was pathetic. I could just imagine all of April's snob friends snickering at the stupid girl in the blue jeans who could barely stay on her horse.

I hardly ever cry, but my eyes were getting very blurry as Thunder and I left the ring in total humiliation and disgrace.

Then I heard April and Shadowfax being called. I stopped just outside the stable area and forced myself to watch.

April and Shadowfax seemed to move in perfect unison. They didn't just jump — they flew. One fence after another. A clear round, which is what they call it when you have no knockdowns and no refusals. When they were through, the crowd stood up and cheered.

I was slumped on a bale of hay in Thunder's stall when M and my friends found me.

"Hey, Randy," Sabrina said, trying her best to be cheerful. "You guys looked great!"

The only thing worse than being humiliated is having people pity you afterward. All I could manage to do was sigh.

"That was a hard course," M said. "Everyone

missed at least one jump."

"Except April," I said under my breath.

"Well, yes." M patted my head, which just made me feel worse.

"At least it's over," I said. "Now I don't have to go to the regionals and do it all over again in front of D."

"Um, actually, Randy . . ." Al began.

I looked up, hoping I didn't look like I'd been crying.

"Actually, what?" I demanded.

"Actually, just before we got here, we heard them announcing the riders who had qualified to go to the regionals. There were a total of twelve contestants today, and the top seven get to go on. You qualified."

At least Al knew me well enough to realize that this news would not make me jump for joy.

"What number was I?"

Allison looked at M and then looked away.

"Honey —" M began.

"What number was I?" I repeated.

"You were number seven," M said finally.

Chapter Seven

"It's okay, boy," I whispered as I groomed Thunder, trying not to sound as down as I felt. "You were great. It was my fault."

Thunder was hot and a little muddy after the workout of jumping the prelim course. I had to get him cleaned up and cooled down before we could load him back onto Mr. Cole's horse trailer for the trip back to Acorn Falls.

I was whispering because April and Shadowfax were just a few stalls away. April was chattering on happily to her father and her coach. Of course, they were all thrilled that she had come in first in the prelims. The competition would be tougher at the regionals, but it was a really good start.

M and my friends were all waiting out by our car. I guess they realized I didn't want to spend a lot of time talking right then. Besides, it was too hard to listen to everybody telling me how things really weren't so bad.

"Thunder about ready?" Richard asked as he walked up and stroked Thunder's head. He and Duke had finished second in their class a little earlier.

"Yeah," I said flatly.

"I saw your run," Richard said.

"You're not about to tell me how great it was, are you?"

Richard shrugged. "Why would I tell you that? You were lousy."

I almost smiled. Somehow it felt better just having someone admit the truth. "Yeah, I am."

"I didn't say you *are* lousy, I said you *were*. You've got basic talent as a rider. A lot of people don't, but you do."

"Thunder's the one with the talent," I said glumly. "I didn't do anything but get in his way and drag him down with me."

"Well, you need to practice a lot more before the regionals, that's for sure. And you only have one week."

"Yeah, right. Practice," I said as I carefully worked the dandy brush along Thunder's coat, starting at the head and working toward the tail.

Richard looked like he was going to say something else, then he shrugged and walked away.

The ride home to Acorn Falls was not exactly fun. In fact, it was a lot like a funeral I went to once. Nobody said anything, and we just pretty much listened to the radio.

We dropped everyone off at their homes, then headed home ourselves. I went straight upstairs and flopped onto my bed.

All I kept seeing over and over again in my mind was that sixth jump. And I kept hearing April's words. It was like she was psychic or something. She'd known that was where I would blow it. She had been totally confident that Thunder and I could not handle that jump.

How had she known? Was I just so obviously bad that she could easily judge which jump would be too hard for me?

The other image that kept coming to mind was of all those horsey people laughing at the girl in the wrong clothes who kept screwing up. I hadn't actually seen any of those people laughing at me, but it was easy enough to imagine. I could guess what they were thinking. At least if I had been wearing their uniform, maybe they wouldn't have noticed me so much.

I wallowed in depressing, frustrating thoughts

like that for a while, just digging my way further and further into this hole of depression. It was starting to feel like one of the worst days of my life. Then M called upstairs.

"What?" I shouted grouchily.

"Telephone."

I couldn't believe any of my friends would be dumb enough to call me. They all knew me well enough to know they should keep their distance when I'm down.

"Tell them to leave a message," I yelled.

"It's your father," M called back.

I groaned. Great. All I needed now was to hear how much D was looking forward to coming and watching me in the regionals. Me, the last person to qualify.

I climbed off my bed reluctantly and headed downstairs. The phone was lying on the table. M had split to her studio. She knows me well enough to keep her distance, too.

"Hi, D," I said, not even trying to sound cheerful.

"Hi, Ran," D said. I could tell from the hollow sound on the line that he was calling from the cellular phone in his car.

Suddenly I had this image of him driving

through the streets of Manhattan, stuck in traffic, with all the cabdrivers honking their horns while he sat there with the phone in his ear. I would have given anything to be back in New York right then, miles away from prelims and regionals and the total humiliation of the day.

"What's up?" I asked.

"Well, I may have some bad news," D said. "May, I said. It's not definite. But since you and I have an agreement that I will not tell you I can do something and then pull a no-show, I thought I should warn you up front."

"What's this all about?" I wasn't really tracking. Probably because all I could really think about was that stupid competition.

"What I'm trying to tell you, honey, is that I'm not sure I can make it to the competition in Minneapolis. I can probably still make it, but there's a chance that a commercial shoot I have scheduled will run a day longer than I had planned. The sports star who is appearing in it may be in an extra playoff game."

I didn't say anything, because to tell the truth, a big part of me was actually glad to hear this news. And another big part of me felt lousy for being relieved that I was going to miss a chance to see my dad.

"I know you're disappointed, Ran, and you know I'd love to be there — "

"No biggie, D," I said quickly. "Really."

"Listen, I'm still going to try very hard to make it."

"I know, D," I said.

"Either way, good luck. And — oh, darn. Listen, I'm coming up on the tunnel. This phone won't work in there, so I'd better sign off now."

"Cool, D," I said.

"I love — " All of a sudden the line turned to static.

I put the phone down. "I love you, too, D," I said.

"Before I forget, here's the videotape of the preliminaries," Sabs said Monday, leaning across the lunch table to hand me a videocassette.

"You keep it," I said nonchalantly. "It might be good for some laughs."

"But you'll need it to see what you did wrong and try to improve," Sabs pointed out.

"I know what I did wrong," I said, managing to laugh dryly. "Everything."

"You qualified," Katie offered as she opened

her milk carton.

"I qualified at the absolute bottom," I replied.

"So what? It's like the wild-card team in professional football. They're the last team to qualify, but sometimes they go on and win the Super Bowl."

Count on Katie to be prepared with some uplifting sports analogy.

"This isn't football," I said. "Anyway, can we talk about something else?"

"Look, if you're going to be involved in any sport, you're going to have bad days," Katie continued. "You learn from your mistakes and get back in there."

"Thanks for the pep talk, coach," I said with a sigh.

"I thought I would help Sabs videotape you again this afternoon," Al said. "You *are* going to practice this afternoon, aren't you?"

I shrugged. I'd been trying to avoid bringing this up, but it looked like my friends were going to make me deal with it.

"No need to practice," I said at last, putting on a casual expression. "I'm not going to the regionals."

"What?" Sabs demanded. "What do you mean?"

"Hey, it's no big deal," I said. "I never said I was going to devote my whole life to riding horses or anything. I tried it out. But it's just not my kind of thing. I mean, for a start, it's totally about being a snob."

"I thought it was about loving horses," Al said quietly.

"That's what I thought, too," I replied, feeling a little frustrated that we couldn't just let the whole thing drop. "But all the dumb clothes and the rituals and saluting the judges and all — not to mention bragging about your horse's pedigree. Give me a break! That's not me. I'm into hard rock and the most out-there styles and doing things my own way."

"I thought you were into riding, too," Al persisted. Al can be annoying sometimes, when she doesn't just accept whatever you tell her. She keeps at you and keeps at you until you tell her the truth.

"But isn't your dad coming to see you in the regionals?" Sabs asked.

I shook my head. "No, I don't think so. He called to say he might not be able to make it. That

means he definitely won't be there. Which is perfect," I said firmly, "because I won't be there,
either."

Chapter Eight

That afternoon after school, we were all going to head to Fitzie's, but at the last minute I just didn't feel like it. Instead, I hopped on my skateboard and cruised around for a while. I knew my friends would understand. Sometimes I just have to be by myself to clear out my head.

I wasn't even really thinking about where I was heading, but eventually I looked up and saw that I was near the edge of town on the road that leads to Rolling Hills Stables.

I shook my head. No way was I in the mood to go there. I turned my board around and was about to head toward town. I was hoping that my friends were still at Fitzie's.

Just then I heard this loud whinny, carried on the breeze.

Now, of course, all horses sound pretty much the same. But I had the definite feeling that this particular whinny belonged to Thunder.

I stopped and listened. The sound came again, far away, but clear. It was almost like he was calling to me because he knew I was close by. Ridiculous, maybe, but that's how it seemed.

"Okay, okay," I grumbled as I turned my board back toward the stable. "I'll come and see you."

A few minutes later I was at the stable. I saw Richard off across the field digging a posthole. Farm kids really have to work hard.

As soon as I got to Thunder's stall, he gave me this impatient, what-took-you-so-long look.

"What's the matter, boy?" I asked, stroking his muzzle. "Did you think it was time for us to practice? Is that what it is?"

Thunder couldn't exactly say yes. I mean, he's smart, but he's not Mr. Ed. Still, I was sure he was waiting for me to take him out — like I had been doing just about every day for the past couple of weeks.

What could I do? Refuse? When he was looking at me with those great big brown horse eyes?

"Okay," I said at last. "But no jumping. That should be a relief, huh? Just a nice easy run around the field. We'll say hello to Richard, then it's back here for a big helping of oats."

I saddled Thunder up, deliberately not choosing the jumping saddle from the tack room. We trotted around the grassy field for a while, but Thunder kept pulling toward the jumping practice ring.

"No! We're done with that," I said firmly.

I headed him off across the field toward the spot where Richard was unloading fence posts from the back of his dad's ancient pickup truck.

"Oh, you like this, do you?" I said to Thunder as he took off happily in Richard's direction. He wasn't pulling toward the jumping area anymore. I assumed he was just happy to see Richard. I didn't even suspect what was really going on in his stubborn horse brain till it was too late.

As we galloped straight toward Richard, he stood up in the back of the pickup and waved at us.

Suddenly Thunder dropped from a full gallop into a canter. It was an odd thing to do, because Thunder loves to run, and the canter is the pace he uses only when he's —

Jumping!

I pulled back on the reins, but Thunder had the bit in his teeth and had decided to completely ignore me. We were coming straight at the pickup truck, which, I had to admit, did look an awful lot like a spread fence.

"No way!" I yelled at Thunder.

I saw Richard's eyes go wide as he realized what was about to happen. He dived for the bottom of the truck just as Thunder tucked up his front legs, drew his rear legs up to give him maximum power, and sprang into the air.

It all happened in a flash. Suddenly everything was quiet as we flew through the air. Flew right over the back of the truck. Flew right over poor Richard, who was flat on his face.

Without even thinking, I adjusted my weight at just the right point on the takeoff and at just the right point on the landing.

"Are you nuts?" I heard Richard shouting as we cantered around in a circle.

"It wasn't my idea!" I shouted back. I pulled Thunder to a stop beside the truck as Richard climbed to his feet, dusting his jeans off.

"What do you mean, it wasn't your idea?"

I shrugged. "Thunder got the bit in his teeth and took off."

"Didn't he get enough jumping over in the practice ring?"

"I didn't take him into the practice ring. I'm

just here to ride, not to practice."

"What are you talking about?" Richard asked quizzically. "You'd better be practicing every chance you get."

I shook my head. "No need. I'm not going to the regionals. I decided to blow it off."

Richard looked at me like I was crazy. Then, slowly, his expression turned to disappointment. I actually had to look away.

"You're bailing out because you did poorly at the prelims?"

"No, I just decided I'm not into all the baloney. All the rules and the clothing and the whole horsey thing, you know?"

"No, I don't know." Richard looked at me doubtfully. "I can't believe you would blow this just because you don't want to wear jodhpurs. That's the stupidest thing I've ever heard in my life."

"It is not!" I said hotly.

"Yes, it is. Look, I know a lot of horse people can be pains in the neck, and I know there are a lot of snobs. But who cares? You can't let the snobs intimidate you."

"I am not intimidated."

"Bull. You let people like April get to you. You

let her convince you that you don't belong."

I didn't really have an answer for that. Probably because I knew in my heart he was right.

Richard rolled his eyes. "I can't believe you, of all people, let her pull that snob act on you. You know, maybe it's my fault. I probably should have warned you about people like her."

"What do you mean, people like her?"

"Well, let me guess. She made some snobby remark about your clothes, right? And she probably did something like tell you that a certain jump was impossible, right?"

I stared at him with my mouth open. "How did you know?"

"Give me a major break. I've been in a lot of these competitions. Most of the competitors are really cool, but you always have one or two who want to try to play head games with you."

"Head games?" I repeated.

"You know — try and distract you, shake your confidence."

I nodded slowly. So that's what April had been up to. And it had worked. Perfectly. She had completely rattled me. Made me doubt I should even be in the competition. Still, that wasn't all of it.

"Look, maybe April did play games with me,

but that still doesn't change the fact that she has a coach and I don't. Or that she — and a lot of the other riders — have more experience than I do. Or that those officials probably won't even let me ride without wearing one of those awful outfits."

Richard shrugged. "It's your choice. You want to quit, fine. Only you're not the only one who should have a vote in deciding." He turned away and began tossing fence posts over the side of the pickup onto the ground.

"Who — " Suddenly I knew exactly who Richard was talking about.

I backed Thunder away from the truck and then held the reins loosely. "Okay, Thunder. What's your vote?"

Without hesitation, Thunder took off at a dead run toward the practice ring.

"What's with you, Randy?" Sabs demanded as we left school the next Friday afternoon. "You haven't wanted to go to Fitzie's with us all week. It was one thing when you had to practice, but now I don't get it."

"Maybe she's turned into one of the horsey snobs," Katie teased.

"I've just been busy," I said.

"Busy doing what?" Sabs asked.

"Busy," I said mysteriously.

I hadn't told any of my friends, but I'd been practicing with Thunder all week. It wasn't that I was trying to keep it a big secret or anything, it was just that after changing my mind before, I didn't want to have to explain why I had changed it all over again, particularly if I still decided not to go to the finals.

Also — and I know this sounds strange — it was like this was just between me and Thunder.

"Actually," I said, "if you guys can pass on Fitzie's today, I really need to go shopping. Want to come with me to the mall?"

"Sure you're not too *busy*?" Katie said in a teasing tone.

"We wouldn't want to cut into your *busy* schedule, Ran," Al chimed in.

"Give me a break," I groaned.

Of course, they finally agreed to go along. I knew that Katie and especially Sabs would never, ever turn down the chance to shop. And they also wanted to see if I had gone totally nuts.

I refused all their inquiries until we were there. Then I very calmly led them to Cowgirl Blues.

"Here? What are you coming here for?" Sabs

asked. "I mean, I love the shop, but — "

Suddenly Al laughed happily. "You're going, aren't you?"

"Going where?" Katie asked.

"She's going to the competition. That's where you've been all week, isn't it? You've been practicing."

I just smiled back. "I wanted to see if I was really going to have the nerve to go through with it before I told you."

"Of course you have the nerve," Al said, patting my shoulder. "You're about the bravest person I know."

"Thanks," I said gratefully. "But there is one thing I don't have the nerve to try unless you guys are all there to help me."

"What's that?" Sabs asked.

I took a deep breath and headed into Cowgirl Blues. Then I marched straight up to Philippa and reached into my pocket. I took out a note from M and a little plastic card and held them out to her.

"My mom's credit card, and a permission note from her," I explained. "I'm all yours, Philippa."

We all had to be up really early Saturday morning. The competition was in Minneapolis, and it started at nine sharp. Al, Sabs, and Katie all slept over so they'd be ready to go with us. Richard and his dad had agreed to take care of transporting Thunder again.

I waited till everyone was downstairs eating breakfast. Then I sneaked back up to my room. I wanted to do what I had to in private. It took about ten minutes, but when I headed back downstairs, everyone stopped talking at once.

M, Al, Sabs, Katie — they were all just staring at me, with their mouths hanging open in disbelief.

"Go ahead and laugh and get it over with," I growled, clumping down the stairs in my knee-high leather boots.

"You look — " Sabs began.

"Watch it," I threatened, waving my new riding crop at her.

"No, you really look great," Sabs said sincerely.

"Honey, you look like you should be riding to hounds with the Prince of Wales," M gushed.

"Then I'd have to wear a red coat, M," I pointed out. "At least this one is basic black."

"Your color," Katie pointed out, laughing.

"One more thing," I said, gritting my teeth. "I

. . . I need some help."

"For what?" Katie asked.

"I need to . . ." I paused to shudder. "I need to braid my hair."

Chapter Nine

"Every horse on the planet must be here," Sabs said when we arrived at the regionals in Minneapolis.

"Or at least every horse in Minnesota," Al added.

It seemed like there were a thousand horse trailers parked in the contestant parking area. Horses were everywhere — practicing jumps, being led from their travel trailers toward the stables, or just cantering around the grounds to let off steam.

I knew this was a major deal, but I really hadn't realized how major. There were riders competing from five states surrounding Minnesota, and show jumping was just one of the events. Most people were there for dressage, which is sort of like ballet for horses. There was a steeplechase event, too. That's a cross-country race on a course with lots of hedges and ditches to jump. Of course, most peo-

ple were just there to watch, or to buy or sell horses.

Fortunately, Thunder had already been
assigned to a numbered stall, so it didn't take too
long to find him. Duke was in the stall beside
Thunder's, and Richard was carefully checking
his horse over, making sure his shoes were good
and clean, and looking for last-minute problems.

"Hey, Randy," he said, not even looking up
from his careful inspection of Duke's left rear
hoof.

"Hi, Richard," I said. Then I reached over to
stroke Thunder's muzzle. "Hey, Thunder. Are you
psyched for this, boy?"

No answer. He just flicked at a fly with his tail,
looking a little bored. I was kind of glad to see he
was taking it all so well, since I was plenty nervous enough for both of us.

"Well, is there anything we can do to help you
get ready?" M asked.

"No, thanks," I said. "You guys should try to
find something to entertain you, I guess. We won't
start the first round for a while, and I need to get
Thunder warmed up and ready to go."

"They have a food tent," Richard offered help-
fully. "And I saw some folks setting up tents to sell

souvenirs and things."

"Shopping?" Sabs asked brightly. "Do you mean there's shopping here?"

Al groaned. "Are you sure we can't help you with anything, Randy?" she asked hopefully.

"Sorry, Al. Look on the bright side — at least it's not the mall."

M came over and put her hand on my shoulder. "You know that however you do, I'm very proud of you."

I just kind of shrugged, but I knew from M's smile that she understood how much her words meant to me.

"Yeah, good luck, Ran," Al added.

"Good luck, Randy! We'll be watching," Sabs said. "And good luck to you, Thunder."

"Be cool," Katie said, giving me a thumbs-up sign.

"Always," I answered, grinning.

There was a lot to do before I could take Thunder out to the collecting ring for his warm-up. First I wanted to walk the course and see what we were going to be up against.

"You going out to do a walk-through?" Richard asked.

I nodded. "I want to be careful this time and

really be ready."

"Take your time. These things always run late, anyway."

At first I could barely pay attention to the course itself. I was too busy being amazed by the number of people in the stands. Already there were thousands of spectators there. I realized as I looked out over the crowd that although there were a lot of snooty horsey types, there were a lot more people who'd just come with their families to have a good time. That made me relax a little.

The course was much tougher than the one at the preliminaries had been. Not only were the jumps a little higher, but they were organized in a more complicated pattern, which required all sorts of tight turns.

My first reaction was to think, No way am I going to make it through this. But then I started concentrating on the specific details — how many paces there were between one fence and the next, how wide the splits were, and exactly how tight the turns were. That kept me so busy that I forgot how nervous I was — for a while, anyway.

I looked each fence over carefully, then closed my eyes and imagined being on Thunder. I thought about exactly what pressure I would apply with my legs, and where I would hold the reins, and what commands I would give him. The more I did it, the less afraid I was.

"Right here," I heard a voice say. "This is where you're going to lose it."

I opened my eyes and wasn't exactly surprised to see April standing there by the fourth fence. "April," I said. "Always nice to see you."

"Nice to see you, Randy," April said, matching my sarcastic tone. "I like your outfit," she added, glancing at my riding costume. "But it takes more than clothes to make a rider. It takes experience to take this jump and set up for jump five. And you can't buy *that* at the mall."

It was so obvious, now that I knew what she was doing. Richard was right. She was up to her old tricks, trying to get me fixated on this one jump so I'd forget everything else.

"Yes, that is a tough jump," I admitted. "And you were so right about the trouble I had at the prelims." I actually managed to smile. "I appreciate your advice."

Naturally, April didn't quite know how to respond to this. She frowned at me, then turned and walked away.

"Hey, April," I called.

She turned back with this impatient expression on her face. "What?"

"Oh, it's nothing. It's just . . . well, I'm not sure I should even say anything, but I know when your birthday is, since I played at your party, and I just happened to be reading the horoscopes this morning, and — "

"And what?"

I shrugged. "Um, never mind. I probably shouldn't even have said anything. Who believes in that stuff, anyway?"

This time I was the one to turn and walk away. April wasn't the only one who could play head games.

By the time I had finished walking the course, I was feeling pretty good.

"Hey, Randy!"

I had to look around for a few seconds to see who was calling me. There were all kinds of people hanging around the railing. Then I saw him.

"D!" I yelled, breaking into a run.

D was standing there with a huge grin on his face. One thing about D — he definitely stands out in the crowd. He's got one pierced ear where he wears a diamond stud, a great ponytail, and he's always decked out in designer suits. No one would mistake him for part of the horsey set. We gave each other a major hug, then I stepped back so he could get the full effect of my "ensemble," as Philippa had referred to it.

"Wow, is this like the height of horsey style or what?" he asked, looking my outfit up and down.

"What can I say?" I answered sheepishly. "I had to do it."

"You look great. Seriously, you know I wouldn't lie. You look fantastic."

I smiled and gave him another hug. "I thought you weren't going to be able to make it."

"I said I might not be able to," he pointed out.

"I'm glad you're here, only . . ." I hesitated.

"Only what?"

"Only it's not like I really have a chance at winning. There are a lot of good riders and great horses here."

D gave me this serious look. "Do you think I came to see you win? I came to see *you* — win, lose, or draw, kid."

"Cool," I said. "Thunder and I will give it a shot."

"I hate to sound like a parent," he said apologetically, "but all I ever expect is for you to do your best. And that's always been great as far as

I'm concerned."

Suddenly I realized I was feeling more relaxed than I had in a long time. D was right. Thunder and I would do our absolute best, and that would be enough. There was never any humiliation or disgrace in trying hard and giving something your very best shot — even if you didn't come in first.

"Well, I've still got some work to do in the stable. I'd better get going," I said. "Where are you going to be sitting?"

"I'll be with your mom and your friends," he said. "I ran into them over by the souvenir stands. Sabrina was buying a cowboy hat."

I laughed. "Sabs is a blue-ribbon shopper. If the competition doesn't start soon, she'll end up buying a horse."

"Good luck," D called as I headed back toward the stables.

I still had lots of work to do with Thunder. First I had to wrap his legs with stretchy cloths called bandages, to help protect his legs in case we hit a fence. Then I put on bell boots, which are these little upside-down cones that protect your horse's hooves.

After that it was time to tack up, which means

putting on the saddle and the bridle, and so on. I was almost done with that when out of the corner of my eye I happened to notice a girl nearby with a beautiful chestnut quarter horse. She was carefully braiding his tail.

I guess she saw me watching, because she turned and smiled at me. "Hi," she said. "My name's Dawn O'Flannery."

"Randy Zak," I replied. Then I pointed at Thunder. "And, of course, Thunder."

"He's a beauty. I've been admiring him. My horse is Charlie."

"He's great," I said sincerely. I nodded at the braid she was working on. "Um, are we supposed to braid?"

"It's not compulsory, but it's sort of traditional," Dawn said. "Would you like me to teach you?"

I shrugged. "You're probably busy."

"Not really."

When she'd completed Charlie's tail, she came over and began work on Thunder, who really adored the attention. There were different kinds of braids — English-style and French-style — and it was all a lot more complicated than I'd imagined. I was glad Dawn volunteered to help me. Luckily, my friends had been around to braid my hair that morning. I wouldn't have known where to start with Thunder's.

"Have you walked the course yet?" Dawn asked as she began to braid Thunder's mane.

"Yes," I admitted. "I'm kind of new at this, but it looked tough to me."

Dawn laughed. "I'm not new at this, and it still looked tough to me. That seventh fence — you know, the rustic rails? Setting up for that is going to be tough."

I eyed her suspiciously. Was she trying to psyche me out, like April? But as she began to discuss different ways we could deal with the problem, I realized that Dawn was really nice. She was actually trying be helpful.

"Well, time for me to head to the collecting ring," Dawn said when we were finished. "Charlie likes a good long warm-up."

"Good luck," I called out.

She grinned back. "You too."

Amazing. She was actually nice. Probably some rider who knew she didn't have a chance, I figured. Unlike April, she didn't have anything to lose by being nice.

Just then Richard appeared, accompanied by

his father. "So, ready to go?" he asked cheerfully.

"Yep. Believe it or not, I am actually looking forward to it."

"Well, I'll be watching. Duke and I aren't on until all you amateurs are out of the ring."

"Amateurs, huh?" I poked him in the arm. "We're going to show you who's an amateur."

"Nice job with Thunder's mane and tail," Mr. Cole remarked.

"A girl named Dawn helped me," I said.

"Dawn O'Flannery?" Richard asked.

"You know her? She seemed really nice."

Richard laughed. "Actually, I don't really know her. I've just seen her around. But everyone says she's a great person. She's also probably the best rider in your class. Next year she's moving up to my class, and believe me, I'm not looking forward to having to compete against her."

So much for my theory that Dawn was only being nice because she didn't have a prayer. Also, so much for my theory that all horse people were snobs.

Before I left, Richard helped me pin my competitor's number onto the back of my jacket. It's this plastic badge that identifies each rider for the judges.

"Thirteen, huh?" Richard said. "Don't let it get to you, okay? It's just a number."

"I am not a superstitious person," I said firmly. "From now on, thirteen just happens to be my lucky number."

I waved to Richard and Mr. Cole and headed to the collecting ring with Thunder. As we trotted past the other competitors, I could tell Thunder was as psyched as I was. He pranced around the ring and bounded over the practice jumps like a real pro.

By the time they called my name, I knew I was ready, and so was Thunder.

Chapter Ten

Show jumpers are divided into different classes, depending on how much experience they've had, but even in my class, there were about fifty riders competing. That meant we had to start off with elimination rounds.

Now, the very best thing to do in show jumping is to perform what they call a clear round — no knockdowns and no refusals. For any knockdown, they give you four faults. If your horse refuses once, it's three faults. On the second refusal it's six points, and if he does it three times, you're out. If you fall off your horse, it's eight faults — not to mention being very embarrassing. The rider with the smallest number of faults wins.

In the first elimination round, Thunder and I jumped a clear round, so naturally I was feeling pretty good. In the second elimination round, we had two knockdowns, but that was still good enough to move us up.

I was already worn out by the time we got to the main event, which was down to ten riders. As they announced the names of the finalists, I was happy to hear my own name coming over the loudspeaker, although it came out as Randy "Sack" instead of Zak. Dawn and April were finalists, too. I was glad when I heard April's name being called, because even though I was totally into the just-do-your-absolute-best thing, I have to admit — I still wanted to kick April's butt in the final round.

"Okay, Thunder," I said as we waited for our turn to compete. "I know you're getting a little tired, but all the other horses are tired, too." I patted his neck. He had been perfectly well behaved, except for trying to ignore my signals on the first jump where we had a knockdown. The second knockdown had been my fault, so we were even.

I watched as the riders made their way through the course, one by one. I tried to concentrate completely, so I could learn from their mistakes. Unfortunately, when it was April's turn, she and Shadowfax didn't make any mistakes. Which meant that to stay in the competition, Thunder and I had to score a clear round, too.

"All right, Thunder. Now's the time. Let's

show everyone what you can do," I said. We saluted the officials and headed for the first fence. Perfect takeoff, perfect landing. On the second fence we were a little late on the takeoff, but we made it. The next four fences were classic, perfect jumps.

"Jump, one, two," I whispered, counting off the paces as we cantered between fences. We struggled a little to turn and set up for jump seven, and as we flew over it, I could hear the faintest nick as Thunder's rear hooves caught the top edge of the fence.

I caught my breath and waited. The rail held firm!

Total relief for me. Another tenth of an inch and we would have been out of it.

"Come on, boy," I urged as we approached the last two fences. They were a breeze. We took them like nothing, and before I knew it, we were cantering away, listening to the sound of applause. I flashed on D giving me a thumbs-up from the stands, and saw my friends applauding wildly.

"I guess we're still in it, Thunder, old boy," I said as we left the ring triumphantly. "Good job!"

Five of the riders jumped a clear round — me, April, Dawn, and two guys. Dawn came riding up beside me as we waited in the collecting ring. "Nice work," she said enthusiastically. "That's a great jumper you have there."

"You didn't do so badly yourself," I said.

"Now it's time for the jump-off. What they'll do is shorten the course, and probably take out the last couple of fences."

"So they make it easier?"

Dawn grinned. "It's fewer fences, but they make each one higher. Plus, you're racing the clock. Fastest clear round wins."

I took a deep breath. Since I hadn't expected to make it this far, I hadn't really thought much about the jump-off part of the tournament. Whatever relief I'd felt at staying in it was replaced by a fresh wave of stomach flutters.

One of the guys was the first to start. I was scheduled last — good news, because I could get a feel for the other riders' mistakes, and hopefully avoid them.

The first guy had two knockdowns because he was trying to get his horse to go too fast.

Next up was Dawn. I hadn't really gotten a chance to watch her and Charlie before, and I have to admit, I was totally blown away. Not only was she a nice person, but she looked like one of those riders who could be Olympic material someday. Naturally, she jumped a clear round with a great time.

Next came the second guy, who jumped clear but kind of slow. So far, it was no contest. Dawn was ahead by a mile.

Then I saw April getting ready on Shadowfax. She had to come right past me to reach the gate. I could see from her face that she was worried.

For a moment I actually enjoyed that look of fear on her face. Then, for some dumb reason, I called out her name.

She glanced over at me, her eyes narrowed. I think she was too distracted to remember that she didn't like me. "What?" she asked.

"Good luck," I said.

Hey, what can I say? It's the kind of classy thing Dawn would have done.

A faint smile actually flickered across April's mouth. She gave me a little nod and headed into the ring.

It was nice, more or less making up. But I have to admit, I wasn't exactly heartbroken when April scored a knockdown a few seconds later.

Now it was my turn. Our turn.

I looked over at my family and friends, and

around at all the other riders. It was weird, but all of a sudden I wasn't worrying anymore. Suddenly I realized that despite all the intensity and nerves and everything, I was actually having fun. I liked being there with Thunder, trying our best, taking our chances.

I gave him one last pat. "Thanks, Thunder," I whispered. After all, if he hadn't "talked" me into it, I wouldn't have been there today.

"Let's do it, pal," I said, and Thunder took off.

At that moment we were magically transformed into one animal with one brain. We were totally in sync and totally attuned to each other. Every jump, every landing, was perfect.

When we were finished, it was like waking up from a dream. I saw the crowd again and heard the loud applause. Allison, Katie, and Sabs were waving a big banner that read GO RANDY AND THUNDER!

They all came rushing down out of the stands as the judges announced the name of the winner.

No, not Randy Zak and Thunder.

Dawn O'Flannery and her horse, Charlie.

"Second place!" Sabs screamed happily.

"Second place out of like *fifty* riders that started out. That's amazing!" Al said, giving me a hug as I climbed down off Thunder.

Then Dawn came over and we shook hands. "I can't believe you were just six-tenths of a second behind me," Dawn said. "I thought you said you aren't an experienced rider."

"I 'm not," I said, laughing.

She shook her head ruefully. "Well, I hate to think of you and Thunder when you *are* more experienced. That's one great horse you have."

"Actually, he's not really mine. I ride him, but he belongs to Mr. Cole," I explained. "He owns Rolling Hills Stables."

Richard ran over to join us, with D, M, and Mr. Cole right behind him. "This is Richard," I said to Dawn. "His dad owns Thunder."

Richard gave me a look like I was crazy. "What are you talking about, Zak?"

"I was just explaining how your dad really owns Thunder."

Mr. Cole sort of grinned, and D shook his head. "I don't see how that could be," Mr. Cole said. He pulled a piece of paper out of his pocket. "I have this paper right here that says Thunder is the property of one Ms. Randy Zak."

I grabbed the paper out of his hand and stared at it, trying to focus on the words. It was a bill of sale. There was a date on it, and a time. It had been filled out about five minutes earlier. I gazed at the bottom of the page, at the two familiar signatures.

Olivia Zak. Peter Zak.

M and D.

"He's yours, if you want him, honey," M said.

Well, you know how it is. You don't want to burst out crying like some dweeb, but that's basically what I did. I tried to say thank you, but nothing was coming out, so I just hugged my mom and dad. Then I hugged Thunder. Then I hugged each of my friends.

I probably would have gone on just hugging every person and horse around, because I had never been happier in my whole, entire life. Fortunately, Thunder started neighing really loudly right about then.

"See, he's happy, too," Katie said.

I had to smile. "No, I'm afraid Thunder isn't very sentimental."

"What's he making all that noise for, then?" Sabs demanded.

"Well, I'm not exactly fluent in horse talk," I said, "but I'd bet anything he just said that it's time to wrap up all this mushy stuff and go get him something to eat."

Don't Miss
GIRL TALK # 45
SABRINA AND TOO MANY BOYS

I was heading toward the pencil sharpener when I noticed that a cute eighth grader named Shawn Sullivan was looking through the astronomy books. Shawn's not superpopular, but I always thought he was really nice. He has longish blond hair and green eyes, and he's unquestionably one of the smartest guys in the eighth grade.

I didn't think he was that cute when he was in the seventh grade. But he'd gotten really tall over the past year and had stopped cutting his hair so short. He looked like he was even taller than my best friend Allison. And she's five foot seven! I couldn't believe how much he'd changed in one year.

Shawn really *was* cute! I wondered if he remembered me at all. I tried to get his attention by pretending to reach a book on the top shelf.

"Which one do you want?" Shawn finally asked, looking up from the book he was thumbing through.

Now I was stumped. I couldn't even pronounce some of the words in the titles.

"Umm, that one," I said, pointing to a thick astronomy book.

Shawn looked a little surprised, but he took the book down from the shelf for me.

"Girls aren't usually interested in astronomy," he commented, handing me the huge book.

When he did that, he looked straight into my eyes and smiled. I couldn't believe how unbelievably cute he was!

"Hey, you're Mark Wells's sister, aren't you?" Shawn asked.

"Yes, I am," I said.

I was thrilled that he remembered me. That was definitely a good sign. Immediately I tried to recall when his birthday was. Mark was invited to his party last year, and all of a sudden I remembered that it was right before Thanksgiving. That meant that he was a Scorpio! And Scorpio was a water sign, just like my prediction said! I promised myself I wouldn't go horoscope crazy, but this was happening exactly like my forecast said it would.

TALK BACK!
TELL US WHAT YOU THINK ABOUT
GIRL TALK BOOKS

Name _____

Address _____

City _____ State _____ Zip_____

Birthday _____ Mo._____ Year _____

Telephone Number (___)_____

1) Did you like this GIRL TALK book?

Check one: YES_____ NO_____

2) Would you buy another GIRL TALK book?

Check one: YES_____ NO_____

If you like GIRL TALK books, please answer questions 3-5; otherwise, go directly to question 6.

3) What do you like most about GIRL TALK books?

Check one: Characters_____ Situations_____
            Telephone Talk_____Other_____

4) Who is your favorite GIRL TALK character?

Check one: Sabrina_____ Katie_____ Randy_____
Allison_____ Stacy_____ Other (give name) _____

5) Who is your *least* favorite character?

_____

6) Where did you buy this GIRL TALK book?

Check one: Bookstore____Toy store____Discount store____
Grocery store___Supermarket___Other (give name)_____

Please turn over to continue survey.

7) How many GIRL TALK books have you read?

Check one: 0____   1 to 2____   3 to 4 ____   5 or more____

8) In what type of store would you look for GIRL TALK books?

Bookstore_____Toy store_____Discount store_____

Grocery store_____Supermarket_____Other (give name)_____

9) Which type of store would you visit most often if you wanted to buy a GIRL TALK book?

Check *only* one: Bookstore_____Toy store_____

Discount store_____Grocery store_____Supermarket_____

Other (give name)_____

10) How many books do you read in a month?

Check one: 0____   1 to 2____   3 to 4 ____   5 or more____

11) Do you read any of these books?

Check those you have read:

The Babysitters Club_____   Nancy Drew_____

Pen Pals_____   Sweet Valley High _____

Sweet Valley Twins_____Gymnasts_____

12) Where do you shop most often to buy these books?

Check one: Bookstore_____Toy store_____

Discount store_____Grocery store_____Supermarket_____

Other (give name)_____

13) What other kinds of books do you read most often?

_____

14) What would you like to read more about in GIRL TALK?

_____

_____

Send completed form to :
GIRL TALK Survey #3, Western Publishing Company, Inc.
1220 Mound Avenue, Mail Station #85
Racine, Wisconsin 53404

LOOK FOR THESE OTHER AWESOME
GIRL TALK BOOKS!

MORE GIRL TALK TITLES TO LOOK FOR

Nonfiction
ASK ALLIE 101 answers to your questions about boys, friends, family, and school!

YOUR PERSONALITY QUIZ Fun, easy quizzes to help you discover the real you!

BOYTALK: HOW TO TALK TO YOUR FAVORITE GUY